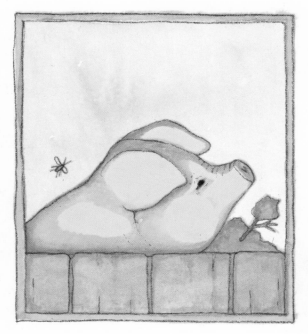

Acknowledgements

Fifteen Bathtubs and *The Tickly Spider* from the book
ANOTHER HERE AND NOW STORY BOOK, edited by
Lucy Sprague Mitchell, copyright 1937 by E. P. Dutton & Co., Inc.,
renewal © 1965 by Lucy Sprague Mitchell, published by
E. P. Dutton & Co., Inc. Used with their permission.

*The Wonderful Kitten, The Shy Little Horse, The Polite Little Polar
Bear, The Steam Roller, The Good Little Bad Little Pig,* and
The Little Girl's Medicine from THE FISH WITH THE DEEP SEA
SMILE by Margaret Wise Brown, copyright 1938 by Margaret Wise
Brown, copyright renewal 1965 by Roberta B. Rauch — *How the
Animals Took a Bath* from JACK AND JILL Magazine, copyright
1939, renewal © 1967 by Curtis Publishing Company, Inc.
Reprinted by permission of Roberta B. Rauch.

Margaret Wise Brown's
WONDERFUL STORYBOOK

25 Stories and Poems
Illustrated by J. P. Miller

A GOLDEN BOOK • NEW YORK

Western Publishing Company, Inc.,
Racine, Wisconsin 53404

Contents

The Green Eyed Kitten

ONCE THERE WAS one kitten. There were lots of other kittens, there always are, but there was one kitten smaller than all the others. Fatter than all the others and blacker than all the others. He was all black with two green eyes.

The other kittens got fat, their whiskers grew longer, their claws grew longer, their ears grew longer and their eyes got bigger and they crawled and bounced and were carried off to their new homes — all but the little old kitten. "He's too little," everyone said. So there he was. "He's too black," they said. "He's all black except for his two little grass green eyes." And so he was left at home.

But the little kitten didn't care at all. He was alone with his own cat mother and he slept a lot and now that the other kittens were gone he got lots to eat and baths seven times a day.

    And more purring
And more blinking
And more warm moments
    than he had ever had before
And a catnip mouse.
That little old kitten,
He was always warm as toast,
    merry as a fiddle,
    bright as electricity,
    and quick as a mouse.

Then one day his mother climbed up in a high and windy tree and forgot to come down.

And there was the little old kitten, more and more and more alone.

He caught seven caterpillars and rolled them over. He jumped for a leaf flying through the air and he caught it.

And then he sat down to think, and these are some of the thoughts he thought. They were all cats' thoughts of course because he was a kitten.

His first thought was *warm fur.*

His next thought was *lions are just big cats so when they are little lions they are kittens.*

Then he thought *I have twenty claws, they pick up sticks and can scratch.*

Then he thought *sweet breezes, a hill has a smell and the moon has not, a tree has a smell and so has a stone. You can hear more and smell more when you're all alone, by yourself.*

That is a dignified way to be, thought the kitten. *I am alone.*

And he looked up into the tree, but all he could see was leaves and leaves and leaves and leaves and leaves and leaves and leaves and leaves and they were all green.

    Bugs are little,
    Beetles are big,
    Stars are quiet,
    Airplanes buzz
    Buzz Buzz Buzz
    Bees buzz, flies buzz, dragon flies.

And then his thoughts made him very sleepy, so he went to sleep. He closed his green eyes.

And he dreamed cat dreams.

And his mother climbed down out of the tree.

The Children's Year

SPRING

The wind blows strong across the hill
And slaps the yellow daffodil,
The red feathery trees
And the sharp green leaves
Remind the farmer to plant his seeds
In the brown earth where the old roots stir,
And early in the morning
The small birds sing.

SUMMER

Now in July
To lie in the sweet grass
With the earth so near
That you can hear
The murmur of insects,
Summer sound,
And almost hear the earth turn round
While far away in the still blue sky
A sudden storm goes rumbling by.

AUTUMN

Apples heavy and red
Bend the branches down,
Grapes are purple
And nuts are brown,
The apples smell sharp and sweet on the ground
Where the yellow bees go buzzing around.
And way up high
The birds fly southward
Down the sky.

WINTER

December comes;
The white snow comes again;
It falls softly in the night
White
From the dark blue sky.
It covers the earth that the spring kept green
And summer kept warm.
It covers the earth where the autumn leaves fell
Golden on the ground.
All is white.
All is still.
And Christmas trees shine green as emeralds
With rubies and diamonds and sapphires
On Christmas night.

9

The Shy Little Horse

ONCE UPON A TIME in a barnyard there was a shy little horse. Every time he heard anyone coming, he ran away. Not so the donkey, not so the pig.

The old gray donkey rolled his eyes and lowered his head, put forward his ears, and then he trotted over to see who the visitor was. And the old fat pig, if she wasn't eating, wallowed over to the side of her pen and grunted at the visitor. But the little horse was shy. He kicked up his heels and he lowered his head and he galloped across the fields away from the visitor.

He galloped away and his mother galloped with him to the far end of the field where the grass was wet and green from the stream that flowed there.

Then one day a visitor came to the barnyard. The visitor was a tall man with a mustache.

The donkey saw him coming and ran to the fence and stuck forward his long ears and rolled his big brown jackrabbit eyes. But the visitor didn't pay any attention to the donkey. The old pig blinked at him, and the chickens scratched about as though there were only chickens in the barnyard. But the visitor didn't even see the old pig and the chickens. The visitor was looking at the shy little horse.

And that shy little horse just lowered his head and kicked up his heels and galloped away.

Now this visitor had come just to see the shy little horse. That was why he came to the barnyard. So he climbed the fence and walked across the field after the little horse. But every time the man got near him, the little horse kicked up his heels and tossed his head in the air and away he flew across the field. And his mother galloped with him and stayed by his side.

But the tall man with the mustache knew a lot about shy little horses because he loved them. He had watched horses for a long time. He knew that the shy little horse was also a curious little horse,

10

just chock-full of curiosity. So he just went and lean-ed against the fence and whistled 𝄢♪♪♪ away to himself and didn't look at the shy little horse any more.

Now that funny little horse saw the man do this and he heard him whistling; because the shy little horse had brand new eyes and brand new ears, and he heard and saw everything. He lowered his head and nibbled the green grass. But while he was nibbling he peeked at the man and pricked up his ears to hear the man whistling. The man didn't move and kept on whistling. 𝄢♪♪♪ The shy little horse kicked up his heels and ran farther down the field and nibbled some more grass and peeked at the man. The man didn't move and kept on whistling. Then the shy little horse nibbled some grass nearer to the man. The man didn't move and kept on whis-tling. 𝄢♪♪♪

What a funny man, thought the shy little horse. Why doesn't he chase me and try to get me in a cor-ner and put a halter over my head? The man didn't move and kept on whistling. The little horse nibbled nearer and nearer. The man didn't move and kept on whistling. 𝄢♪♪♪

The shy little horse's mother put forward her ears and looked hard at the man. Then she snorted and whinnied, kicked up her heels, and galloped far away around the edge of the field. The shy little horse tossed his brand new head in the air and gal-loped with her. They circled around the field and stopped even nearer to the man than they had been before and nibbled the green grass. The man didn't move and kept on whistling. 𝄢♪♪♪

By this time the little horse was so curious he was nearly popping inside. He had never seen a man like this before. All the other men had chased him into a corner and caught him and put a halter over his head. The man didn't move and kept on whis-tling. 𝄢♪♪♪ The shy little horse stepped near-er and nearer. He was quite near to the man now, and he stood there ready to leap away and gallop to the far ends of the field. The man didn't move and kept on whistling. The shy little horse nosed nearer and nearer. The whistling tickled his ears in a way he liked. And he liked the man to stand so still he could get a good look at him. And he liked the quiet way of the man.

Then the man moved just a tiny little bit. If the shy little horse hadn't been looking so hard, he wouldn't have seen. The man uncurled his fingers, and on the palm of his hand were two white square lumps. The little horse stood there ready to jump away if the man moved any more. The man didn't move and kept on whistling. ♪ The shy little horse's mother stretched her head forward to make sure that she saw what she saw. For on the man's hand were two white square lumps of sugar. Just what the old horse loved, and her mouth began to water as she thought of the sweet prickly taste of sugar. She had been out in the field nibbling green grass for so long with her little horse that no one had given her any sugar. She stepped nearer to the man, almost right up to him. The man didn't move and kept on whistling. This was a wonderful thing. The old mother horse stepped right up to the man and buried her nose in his hand and took one lump of sugar and stepped back and chewed it. Then she stepped up and took the other lump of sugar. The man didn't move and kept on whistling. ♪ Then after a while he walked out of the field the way he had come and went away.

The next day he came back, and he stood there whistling and he gave the mother horse another lump of sugar. The third day when he came, he walked right over to the mother horse and put a halter over her head and gave her a lump of sugar. Then he led her out of the field, and the shy little horse followed after, close to his mother's side. The man led the mother horse and the shy little horse through the barnyard among the chickens, past the old fat pig who was eating potato peelings, past the

old gray donkey who was eating thistle and staring with his big jackrabbit eyes. The man led the mother horse and the shy little horse right down the road where the little horse had never been before. His brand new hooves made a clicking noise on the road as he trotted along beside his mother. And the shy little horse was delighted.

Way down the road they went, until they came to a small dirt road. The man turned up the dirt road, and the shy little horse's brand new hooves didn't make clicking noises any more on the dirt, they just made soft little thuds. They went up the dirt road to a long white house with a big white stable with green doors and windows, all green and white. And there were buckets painted green and white, too, in stripes.

And out from the house came a shy little boy and he looked at the shy little horse.

For the tall man with the mustache was the father of the shy little boy, and he had bought the shy little horse for the little boy's very own. The little boy's mother came out of the house and said what a beautiful young horse it was. And the little boy said, "Some day I will ride him."

It wasn't so long before the shy little boy had taught the shy little horse to eat sugar out of his own hand. And the shy little horse and the shy little boy grew up together, and it wasn't long — maybe a year or two, for there was plenty of time — before the little boy had grown old enough to ride the shy little horse and the shy little horse had grown large enough to carry the little boy on his back.

They rode all over the country, they jumped fences and galloped across the green grassy fields, the boy and his horse. And after a while they weren't even shy any more.

The Seven Weathers

One day a little dog had to stay indoors
because he hated to get his feet wet and

That was the day it rained

and the fog rolled in

and it snowed

and the fog melted

14

and there was a tornado

and a hurricane

and a breeze

and a shower.

Then the sun came out
and all the flowers came up because it was
spring.

And then the sun shone and the little dog went
out to take a walk before nightfall on his
four soft feet, just in time —

Because then the stars came out and it was
night
And the wind began to blow all sorts of lovely
evening smells to his nose.

The Good Little Bad Little Pig

POOR LITTLE PIG. He lived in a muddy pigpen, in an old pigpen of garbage and mud, with four other little pigs and an old mother sow. He was a little white-pink pig, but the mud all over him made him look pink and black and gray-pink.

Then one day a little boy named Peter asked his mother if he could have a pig.

"What!" said Peter's mother. "You want a dirty little bad little pig?"

She was very surprised.

"No," said Peter. "I want a clean little pig. And I don't want a bad little pig. And I don't want a good little pig. I want a good little bad little pig."

"I never heard of a clean little pig," said Peter's mother. "But we can always try to find one."

So they sent the farmer who owned the pig a telegram:

TELEGRAM

FARMER, FARMER, I WANT A PIG.
NOT TOO LITTLE AND NOT TOO BIG,
NOT TOO GOOD AND NOT TOO BAD,
THE VERY BEST PIG
THAT THE MOTHER PIG HAD.

The farmer read the telegram, and then he went out to the pigpen and looked at the five little pigs. Three little pigs were fast asleep. "Those," said the farmer, "are good little pigs." And one little pig was jumping all around. "That," said the farmer, "is a bad little pig." And then he heard a little pig squeak, and then he heard a little pig squeal. But when he looked, there was just one little gray-pink pig standing on an old tin pan in the corner of the pen. "That," said the farmer, "is a good little bad little pig." And he reached in and grabbed the little pig by the hind legs and put him in a box and sent him by train to Peter.

When the express man brought the little pig to Peter's front door, his mother said, "What a dirty little pig!"

And the pig said, "Squeak squeeeeeeeeeeeeee ump ump ump."

And Peter said, "Wait till I give this little pig a bath."

But when they let the little pig out, he ran all over the room squealing like a squeaking pig.

"What a bad little pig!" said Peter's father, and he had to catch the little pig by the hind legs to make him hold still while Peter put the red leather dog harness around the little pig's stomach.

16

"Wait," said Peter, "until the little pig knows us. He is not a bad little pig." And he clipped a red leather leash on the little pig's harness.

The little pig stared at Peter out of his blue squint eyes, and then he shook himself and trotted after Peter on the leash.

"What a good little pig!" said Peter's mother, as she came into the room with a pan of bread and milk for the little pig to eat after his journey.

"Wait," said Peter. "Remember this is a good little bad little pig."

"Galump gump gump gump." The little pig was eating. He seemed to be snuffling and sneezing into his food as he ate.

"What a bad little pig!" said the cook, who had come in to see how the little pig was enjoying bread and milk. "What terrible eating manners he has!"

"But he does enjoy his food," said the little boy.

"Yes," said the cook, "he does enjoy his food." And she beamed with a smile all over, for the cook did dearly love for anyone to enjoy his food. "What a good little pig," she said. "He has eaten up everything in the pan."

"Come on, you good little bad little gray-pink pig," said Peter. "I will give you a bath so you will be a clean little white-pink pig."

So Peter and his mother and his father and the cook all went into the bathroom and put the little pig right into the bathtub and let the warm water run all over him.

Peter's mother held his front legs and his father held the little pig's hind legs, so that the little pig couldn't kick himself or the people who were bathing him. The little boy took a big cake of white soap and rubbed it all along the pig's back until he was all covered with pure white soapsuds. Then he took a scrubbing brush, and he scrubbed and he scrubbed right down through the bristles on the little pig's back to the little pig's skin. He scrubbed and he scrubbed until the pure white soapsuds were all black and gray. Then he poured warm water over the pig's back until there was no soap on it. Then he put some more soapsuds all over the little pig's back. And he scrubbed and he scrubbed and he scrubbed and he scrubbed and he scrubbed until the pure white soapsuds were all gray and black again. Then he rinsed off the pig's back with warm water and put more soapsuds on. But this time the soapsuds stayed almost pure white. So he left it on the little pig's back and washed his stomach and his feet until he was all clean and white and pink from the tip of his

17

tail to the tip of his nose. Then they dried the little pig with a great big bath towel, and Peter took him for a walk in the sunshine.

"Look," said Peter as he showed his little pig to the policeman on the corner. "Did you ever see such a fine little clean little pig?"

"I never did," said the policeman, "see such a good little pig." And he blew his whistle and stopped all the automobiles so that Peter and the little pig could get across.

But the little pig did not want to get across, and he pulled back on the red leather leash and refused to budge. Peter pulled and he pulled, but the little pig would not go across the street.

"What a bad little pig!" said the people in the automobiles, and they began to honk their horns. And the little pig began to squeal and squeak. "Squeak squeeeeeeee ump ump ump." But the policeman held up his hand and wouldn't let the automobiles go. Then he came over to Peter and his pig.

"You pull him, Peter," he said, "and I'll get behind him and push." So they did. And when they got to the middle of the road, the little pig trotted on after Peter just as nicely as you please. "What a good little pig," said the people on the other side of the street.

And so it was that Peter got just what he wanted. A good little bad little pig. Sometimes the little pig was good and sometimes he was bad, but he was the best little pig that a boy ever had.

18

The Boy Who Belonged to the Cat

ONCE THERE WAS a little boy and he belonged to a cat and was brought up by a cat and he was the healthiest, happiest little boy in the world.

Instead of opening his eyes slowly in the morning, he blinked them open. So did the cat.

And then they began to stretch and to yawn. The cat shot out one leg and spread the pads of her paws. So the boy shot one foot forward in bed and spread his toes. He spread his fingers. Then he shot out his other leg and stretched his toes and at the same time on the end of his arms he stretched all his fingers out like cat paws or starfish and yawned again. Then he stretched his little stomach and back and got up.

And while the cat washed her eyes and her whiskers with her tongue and her paw, he washed with a big wet wash rag.

Then they went out and sat and dried themselves in the warm sun and blinked at the world and thought their first thoughts without a word. And the sun shone on them and warmed their bones.

Then they were hungry and they both drank their milk.

And some mornings they would have a little fish.

At noon the cat gave the little boy green vegetables because he didn't like green grass and the cat didn't really care whether she ate hot green string beans or cold green grass. But the boy did.

Then after lunch the cat found a quiet place, curled in a warm ball, purred a little and fell asleep. All day long whenever the cat or the boy had nothing to do or had done too much, they would take these little cat naps — why not?

All the better to grow on, purred the cat.

So the cat taught the little boy to watch quietly and to sit in the sun and to keep out of big smells and big noises and big crowds. And he was the happiest, healthiest little boy in the world and very glad that he belonged to a cat.

19

The Little Toy Train

In the little green house lived a cat and a mouse,
a girl and a boy,
and a man with a little toy train.
One day the train ran away.
It was a very little train.
So it ran down a mouse hole.
And the cat and the mouse
and the girl and the boy
and the man who were all very little too
ran down the mouse hole after the
little toy train.

And the little toy train ran far away following rabbit tracks in the
grass until it popped down a rabbit's hole and woke up seventeen
little rabbits who went right back to sleep again until
the cat
and the mouse
and the girl
and the boy
and the man
came running after the little toy train
and woke all seventeen little rabbits
up again.

20

And so the seventeen little rabbits ran after the little toy train
And the little toy train ran on and away
    through a field of clover and timothy hay,
        through a hole in a tree
            and a hole in a stone
                and a hole in the air
                    near a telephone pole,

    through a log
    and a pond
    near a big green frog,
        through a keyhole into a baker's shop
    and on
        and on
            without a stop
    followed by seventeen rabbits
        a man
            a boy
                a girl
                    a cat
                        and a mouse
Until it came to the little green house and ran home again,
And that was the trip of the little toy train.

The Little Flat Flounder

ONCE THERE WAS a little flat flounder with two eyes on the top of his head who lived in the depths of the sea.

Around was green water and under the water was sand and seaweed and a few dark rocks where the blue-black lobsters crawled, slowly opening and shutting their claws.

From their long stalked beady black lobster eyes they looked into the cold blue eyes of the flounder and the dark gray-blue eyes of the cod and the pollack and haddock, and into the brown-black eyes of the skate, and into the yellow eyes of the mackerel.

Fish never close their eyes.

Even when they sleep, fish never close their eyes.

So there lay the little flounder flat in the sand with his gray-blue eyes wide open, night and day.

He watched for food and he watched for danger.

And the minute the flounder saw the lobster he hid in the soft wet sand.

For the lobster with the snapping claws was no friend of the flounder.

The little flounder had plenty of enemies waiting to dive through the sea to catch him.

It seemed as though everything in the air and in the water was after the little flounder.

They were all after the little flounder.

The fishhawk was after him ready to plunge down on him, down through the water like a rock from the sky.

If he didn't keep well hidden in the sand at low tide, the blue heron was there waiting to dip his long neck down for him.

Or the gulls were swooping to dive for him.

And always the fishhawk would hover, waiting, his two striped wings spread across the air, his sharp bird eye peering down through the waters for the moving shadow that would be a fish. And, of course, he hoped that the fish would be a flounder — a little flat flounder.

But it was not only the hawks and the herons and the gulls that were after the flounder.

The other fish were after him too — the codfish, the dogfish, the skate. The mackerel, the halibut, and the shad.

And the only way for him to escape from them was to hide.

The little flat flounder could make himself so much like the sand and seaweed he lay on that no one could see he was there. Wherever the little flounder humped himself, his coloring changed with the parts of the sea. He was a chameleon of the ocean deep.

The fishermen were after him, too, with hooks and lines and nets, but he stuck to the clams and sea fleas and sand worms on the bottom of the sea for his food.

He sniffed about in the sand until he knew his food was there. Then he flipped along till he caught it. He kept himself full of his own food. And he never went near a baited hook.

Fifteen Bathtubs

ONCE THERE WAS a little boy who lived in a house with fifteen bathtubs in it. And you might think that this little boy was the cleanest little boy in the world with fifteen bathtubs in his house. But he wasn't. He was the dirtiest little boy in the world, because he hated to wash and he never used even one of the fifteen bathtubs. Of course, he did take a bath once a month. But when he did take a bath, what do you think he used? He used the garden hose. When the gardener was spraying the flowers in a soft fine spray of water, this dirty little boy would run right through the hose water; and that was the only way he took a bath except when he took a sun bath. He never got into one of the fifteen bathtubs.

Then one morning when all the creatures in the garden were hopping about, the rabbits and squirrels were hopping about and the chipmunks and woodchucks were hopping about and the bees and the butterflies were flying about, the little boy got up from the table where he had been eating toast on jam for breakfast instead of jam on toast; he smeared the jam across his face with the back of his hand and went out in the garden.

Now this was a very lively morning in the garden. It was a clean shining morning, the kind of a

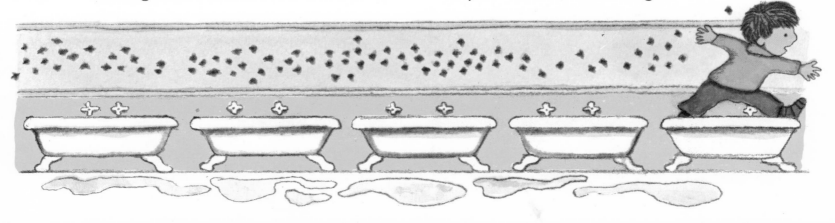

morning that made the animals feel as though they owned the garden. They forgot all about the people that usually frightened them away.

When the little boy ran out into the warm buzzing sunlight, the animals didn't notice him. "Just that dirty little boy," they seemed to say and kept on hopping about; and the flowers kept on growing, and the sun kept on shining, clean and shining.

So the little boy lay down to take a sun bath. He turned his sticky jam-smeared face up to the sky and closed his eyes. The rabbits hopped about and the squirrels hopped about and the woodchucks hopped about all around him, and the butterflies flew and the bees went buzzing all around.

They buzzed in the flowers and they droned through the air, looking for something sweet to make into honey. And then they found the little boy's jam-sticky face. The little boy was asleep. Bzzzzzzzzzzzz. A sticky treasure! Then suddenly many bees were flying all around the little boy's face. Zoom Bzzzzzz Szz zzz zz z. They buzzed about his nose and lips, bzzzz. They buzzed nearer to his cheek. Szzzzz buzzz, after the sticky sweet jam on his face.

The little boy jumped awake, and he jumped to his feet and he jumped away. But the bees came buzzing all around right after him, trying to get the jam off his face. He ran and he ran, but still the bees came buzzing after him. He ran all around the garden, and the bees buzzed all around the garden after him. He ran and he ran into a field, and the bees buzzed through the field after him. He ran and he ran and he ran through a wood, and the bees came buzzing after him. Then he ran and he ran and he ran. Then he ran and he ran down the black tar road, and the bees buzzed down the black tar road after him. He ran and he ran up the gray gravel driveway, and the bees came buzzing up the gray gravel driveway after him. When he got to his house, he ran in the open front door, and the bees came buzzing in the open front door after him; and he ran up the stairs, and the bees came swarming up the stairs after him.

When he got to the fifteen bathrooms, he jumped into one bathtub
   and into another bathtub
      and another bathtub
         and another bathtub
           and another bathtub
         and another bathtub
      and another bathtub
   and another bathtub
into all the fifteen bathtubs fifteen times.

Then the bees flew out the window and back to the flowers in the garden. And they never chased the little boy again, because from that day on he was just as clean as the sunlight.

The Steam Roller

ONCE THERE WAS a little girl and it was Christmas. It was Christmas and her mother and father didn't give her any oranges for Christmas. No dolls. No candy. No new clothes, no books. No sugar plums, no baby carriages. No. They gave her a Steam Roller. A big black steam roller with a silver bell and a brass chimney on it as shiny as gold. Smoke was coming out the chimney and a sort of hissing sound of steam — ssss-wssswwwwwsss.

The little girl climbed up the ladder to the driver's seat, pushed the sticks that made the steam roller go, blew the whistle and rang the bell, and away she went down the road. The big steam roller wheel crushed all the little pebbles on the road and squashed all the big rocks.

Crunch, Crunch, Crunch, it went rolling down the road making everything flat before it. And sssssss a fine smoke of steam came out of its brass chimney and made the steam roller go. There were a lot of buttons to push and sticks to pull. But the little girl didn't know which to push or which to pull to make the steam roller stop.

An old pig went wallowing across the road and blinked its small red eyes.

"Look out, Old Pig," said the little girl. "Get out of my way because I can't stop. Get out of my

28

way or I'll squash you flat."

But the old pig didn't get out of the way. And the steam roller ran right over it and squashed the old pig flat on the road. Flat as a pig's shadow in the middle of the road.

A chicken came fluttering over the road. The little girl blew the whistle. Screeeeeeeeee — up.

"Get out of my way or I'll squash you flat."

And the old yellow chicken got so excited squawking "Which Way Which Way Which Way," and flapping its yellow feather wings, it flew right under the steam roller. Looking back, the little girl saw it flat on the road like the shadow of a chicken or a feather fan.

But the little girl couldn't stop the big steam roller and it went rolling down the road squashing everything in its way. It squashed her mean old aunt flat on the road. It squashed three people she didn't know, it squashed two automobiles and a garbage truck and a trolley car.

Then a policeman stood up in the middle of the road. He held up his hand and blew his whistle. " S T O P ," he said.

"I can't stop," said the little girl, for by this time she had forgotten how to stop. And she ran right over the policeman and squashed him flat on the road with his hand in the air saying S T O P.

The road ahead was clear. No one was on it. No pigs, No chickens, No aunts, No people she didn't know, No automobiles, No garbage trucks, No trolley cars and No policemen. Then along came the little girl's teacher.

"Merry Christmas, little girl," said the little girl's teacher. And the little girl said, "Merry Christmas," but the steam roller wouldn't stop and it squashed the teacher and the book she was carrying, right flat in the middle of the road with a Merry Christmas smile on her face. Flat in the road like a shadow.

Then the little girl saw her friends coming down the road, the children that were just her age, and they called to her saying, "Give us a ride on your steam roller."

"Look out," called the little girl. "I can't stop this steam roller and it will squash you flat."

But the children didn't seem to hear her and they came running toward her. The little girl blew the whistle and rang the silver bell, but still the children came running toward her. "STOP," she called to them. But still they came running.

This will never do, thought the little girl. I can't squash all the children my own age. So she headed the steam roller across a field and then she jumped out of it while it was still going. The steam roller went rolling over the field squashing the fences until they looked like the shadows of fences around the fields. And away it went. The little girl hurt herself on the road when she jumped from the steam roller going full speed. But when she got up she found that she hadn't hurt herself very much. It didn't hurt for long.

The children her own age came running up to her.

"We wanted a ride," they said.

"Oh, no, you didn't," said the little girl. "That steam roller doesn't stop, whatever stick you pull or button you push. And it squashes everything it comes to flat. It would have squashed you all flat if I hadn't headed it off the road into the fields and jumped out."

"Oh," said the children her own age. And they looked after the steam roller. It was just rolling over the last hill. It rolled over the hill and then disappeared into the distance. It rolled off into the ocean and squashed a few fish flat and stopped.

"Well," said the little girl. "I am glad that old

steam roller is gone." And she wished the children a Merry Christmas and ran home to her mother and father.

"Well," said her father, "and how did you like your steam roller ride? And what did you do with your steam roller?"

"At first, it was fun," said the little girl, "but I couldn't stop the steam roller and it squashed everything and everybody it came to flat on the road. And then all the children my own age came running up the road and I couldn't squash them, so I headed the steam roller across the fields and jumped out of it while it was going. And the steam roller rolled away across the fields squashing the fences and went away out of sight. It just rolled away.

"And a pig and a chicken and a policeman all got squashed flat on the road like shadows and I don't know how to get them up again."

"Well," said the little girl's mother and father. "We have another Christmas present for you."

And there at the front door all wrapped up in tissue paper with red ribbons on it was a Giant Steam Shovel.

"Get in that," said her father and mother, "and go scoop up the squashed flat pigs and people and automobiles. Scoop them up out of their shadows and they won't be squashed flat any more."

So the little girl tore off the tissue paper from the steam shovel and away she went down the road. Off she went on the caterpillar steam shovel wheels, and when she came to the pig shadow, *Scoop* she scooped and the old pig grunted up out of its shadow and trotted away. And when she came to the chicken, *Scoop* she scooped it right up out of its shadow; and still cackling Which Way Which Way Which Way, the chicken fluttered away.

And when she came to her mean old aunt and the three people she didn't know, *Scoop* she scooped them right out of their shadows and they all went hurrying down the road.

She scooped up the two automobiles and the garbage truck and the trolley car and off they rattled. And *Scoop* she scooped up the policeman, who raised his other hand and blew his whistle and said Go. Then *Scoop* she scooped up her teacher out of the shadow on the road and her teacher said "Merry Christmas" again and the little girl said "Merry Christmas."

And then all the children her own age came running and she gave them each a ride up in the air in the scoop for the fun of it. *Scoop* she scooped them way high up in the air and then let them down again.

Then she turned the steam shovel around, and off she went home to Christmas dinner.

Count to Ten

(WITH THANKS TO LEAR)

There was once a little owl
  Count to one
1
    1
      one little owl

There were two little trolls
  roly
    poly
      Count to two
2
        1, 2
          two little trolls

There were three little pigs
  piggy
    wiggy
      dance a jiggy
        Count to three
3
          1, 2, 3
            three little pigs

There were four little foxes
  clocksy
    foxy
      doxy
        hide behind the rocks
          Count to four
4
            1, 2, 3, 4
              four little foxes

There were five little fish
  fishy
    squishy
      slishy
        in a dishy
          very swishy
            Count to five
5
              1, 2, 3, 4, 5
                five little fish

Six little pickles
  tickle
    trickle
      sickle
        fickle
          stickle
            crickle
              Count to six
6
                1, 2, 3, 4, 5, 6
                  six little pickles

Seven little drums
  bum little
    rum little
      tum little
        dum little
          hum little
7
            strum little
              some little
                Count to seven
                  1, 2, 3, 4, 5, 6, 7
                    seven little drums

Eight little eyes
  blinky
    thinky
      dinky
        linky
          trinky
            minky
              squinky
                winky
8
                  Count to eight
                    1, 2, 3, 4, 5, 6, 7, 8
                      eight little eyes

32

Nine little noses
  sniffy
    whiffy
     miffy
      piffy
       squiffy
        tiffy
        liffy
         diffy
         biffy
          Count to nine
           1, 2, 3, 4, 5, 6, 7, 8, 9
            nine little noses

9

Ten little kings
  kingy
    ringy
     singy
      dingy
       lingy
        stringy
         flingy
          mingy
           quick and clingy
           wild and wingy
           Count to ten
            1, 2, 3, 4, 5, 6, 7, 8, 9, 10
             ten little kings

10

They Could All Smell It

BUT WHAT WAS IT?

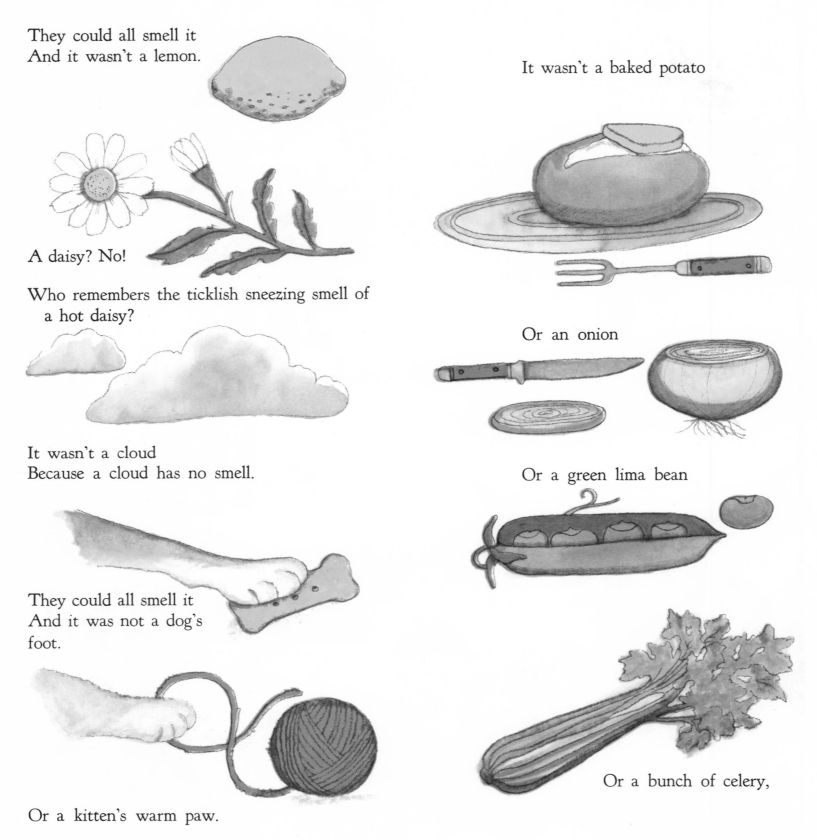

They could all smell it
And it wasn't a lemon.

A daisy? No!

Who remembers the ticklish sneezing smell of
a hot daisy?

It wasn't a cloud
Because a cloud has no smell.

They could all smell it
And it was not a dog's
foot.

Or a kitten's warm paw.

It wasn't a baked potato

Or an onion

Or a green lima bean

Or a bunch of celery,

34

It was not the moon
Because the moon has no smell,
    Nor the moon nor the sun nor the stars.
But they could all smell it coming closer and
    closer and closer.

A bunny has a smell,

And a mirror has not.

What could it be?

Was it a——? No.   Was it a——? No.
Was it a——? No.   Was it a——? No.
Was it a——? No.

What do you think it was?

It was a little old skunk far away

        coming closer

                and closer

                        and closer

                                and closer,

And it wasn't a stone.

Carrying a rose in its mouth.

A fern has a smell,

        And a ruby has not.

The Tickly Spider

A LITTLE BLACK SPIDER lived deep in the grass about three buttercups away from the edge of the field where the little boy was lying on his stomach. The little boy was lying on his stomach peering in between the long green grass blades. Deep, deep, deep in the grassy wilds the little boy looked, even beyond the bright yellow green that the sunlight made as it twisted down the grass blades. And as he watched, he saw strange things. He saw a red lady beetle climbing down a stalk of grass, very slowly taking her time. He saw the shadow of a butterfly that was flying above the grasses. And then——

In and out and around the grass stems came the little black spider. Lugging and puffing along it came, as black spiders come. Over one yellow root and around a brown twig, under a root and over a stick. The black spider was coming straight towards the little boy's nose, just as straight as a spider can come winding in and out of the grasses.

The little boy saw it coming and wondered if it would come all the way up to his nose. He watched it carefully. And as he watched, he saw a ray of sunlight climb down a grass blade to the spider's back, and he got a better look at the spider. He saw little yellow spots on the spider and little furry fuzzy hairs. He saw the dusty gray claws of the very scritchy scrawny spider coming towards him. The spider knew the little boy was there, because with its shiny black eyes it looked right into the little boy's eyes. But the little boy knew just what to do, so he didn't care even if the spider jumped on his nose suddenly. He knew that if you kept stone still and didn't move at all, even wasps and bumble bees wouldn't sting you. So he knew that if he kept stone still, the spider would only walk across him to get into the grass on the other side. He was just like a big hill to the spider, a big hill that had to be climbed to get across to the other side. But if he jumped or jerked, the spider

Then he didn't feel any more tickling. Maybe the spider was gone and was in the grass on the other side of him. But still the little boy lay quiet as a stone. He wasn't sure. After a while, he hadn't felt any more tickly feelings for a long time now, he began to be sure the spider was gone. So he lifted his head slowly; then he turned his head very slowly. It is all right if you move slowly a little bit, just as long as you don't jerk or move suddenly. When he had his head all turned around and his body turned around, too, he looked into the grass on the other side.

At first he didn't see anything. Then he saw the black furry spider crawling off through the grasses, over a root and around a twig, under a root and over a stick, in and out and around the grass stems.

And that was how the little boy stayed very still and saw a lot of things happening around the roots of the grasses.

might think he was not friendly and bite him or sting him. But the little boy knew how to be quiet, so he just lay there stone still. He wasn't brave, he just knew that the spider wouldn't hurt him if he didn't move. He was just a little boy who knew how to be very still.

When the spider came up to the last blade of grass in front of his nose, it stopped. And it looked at the little boy's face. Then it began to climb the tall blade of grass next to the little boy's face. It climbed and it climbed halfway up the grass blade, and it climbed and it climbed until the grass bent towards the little boy's cheek. But it didn't quite touch him. So the spider climbed some more; and when the grass was bending almost all the way over the little boy's cheek, it jumped. Plunk, right in the hollow under the little boy's eye. But the little boy lay very still. Then tickle tickle, the fuzzy old spider started down the little boy's cheek. Tickle tickle, past his nose. Tickle tickle, by the corners of his mouth. The little boy nearly laughed. But he knew better. He lay very still. He didn't even smile. Even though it tickled like a million feathers when the spider climbed down his chin to his neck and went across his neck towards the back, he didn't move or smile.

The Wonderful Kitten

ONCE THERE WERE four little kittens, a little fur pile of kittens. And they lived on a white woolly sheep-skin rug in the clothes closet. When they were born they were as small as a mouse and as big as a bird. They all had whiskers and claws and noses and tiny round ears and tails. But their little eyes were closed tight shut for two weeks, and they didn't have any teeth. All they could do was to kick with their paws in the air and squeak.

Their mother thought they were so beautiful that the minute they were born she began to purr. She purred them a cat song as they lay by her side.

> Purr Purr
> My cat-whiskered mouse
> Come close to my sides
> For this is your house
> Purr Purr
> My Kitten—O—Mouse

Fluff Ball Angel, for that was the mother cat's name, loved her little fur kittens. She loved them with a long steady purr.

Purrrrrrrrrrrrrrr. Purrrrrrrrrrrrrrr. And her eyes were bright and shiny when she purred. She curled up her paws and waved them in the air.

For they were four beautiful round fur kittens in a little fur pile. One little kitten was white as the snow, and one little kitten was gray. One little kitten was black as the night, and one little kitten had yellow stripes on his black coat like a wee baby tiger. They crawled around their mother's sides for a long time.

Then one day after they had had their little blue eyes open for a week, one of them said, "Peep, Peep. What a wonderful kitten I am. I can Yawn some, Sneeze some, Purr some, Lick some, See some, Hear some, and CRAWL. I'm a wonderful cat the size of a rat and I think I will crawl away."

So he waved his four black paws in the air, because he was on his back when he thought about crawling away. But he didn't get anywhere by

waving his paws in the air. He stayed in the very same spot. So then he wiggled and wriggled until he got his fat little stomach to roll over. And there he was on his legs.

Hic-up.

"Fiddlesticks," said the little kitten. "What's that?" And he opened his eyes, his brand new eyes, and looked all about.

Hic

There it went again!

Hic

He looked at all his brothers and sisters. But there they were all curled up sound asleep. What could that noise be?

The Wild Garden

In this garden you will find
No columbine or eglantine.
All the flowers that you will find
Were found by me and they are mine.
You will find white violets from the woods
That I dug up in the Spring,
And you will find daisies from the fields,
And one buttercup.
I planted lots of buttercup seeds
But only one came up.

Here come the bees with a great big buzz,
Yellow and black and covered with fuzz.
Here come the flies in a big black swarm
To tickle a fat little girl's bare arm.

Here come the beetles all shiny and green
And red and yellow and shiny and mean to
    leaves and roots.

Here comes a butterfly first to fly
Out of June and into July.

And here sleeps a sleepy young firefly.

Every spring they come again,
Yellow flowers in the rain,
And lambs are born
And birds are born
In the soft green early morn.

The red bird whistles in the tree.
Spring is here
Endlessly
Ceaselessly
For an instant
In a tree.

Wild strawberries
Are wild,
They taste wild
And their roots run wild
Through the ground,
And they hide like
Little wild red strawberries
In the grass,
And you see them
Suddenly
Small and red
And wild.

The Wonderful Room

THERE WAS a Wonderful Room with a big red bed and a vast gray rug with soldiers and drums on it and a glass fireplace and a big fur chair and a little table with a cake on it and a book with nothing in it and a book with something in it and an ocean outside the window with seven boats sailing on it and a picture on the wall of a horse with a hat on his head and a picture of a panda kicking a panda

and a wooden soldier

and a golden hunting horn

and by the fire in the glass fireplace sat a cat and a dog and a sleepy old owl who lived in this wonderful room and a hole in the wall where a little mouse lived and nobody knew he was there.

And there was a great big hump under the white sheets on the big red bed and who could that be hiding there with one bare foot wiggling its toes sticking out from under the covers?

And over the bed was a light like a star and on the ceiling were starfish that stayed there because they were glued onto the ceiling. And in four little vases were wild flowers and wild flowers and wild flowers, and wild flowers picked from a field at noon — buttercups, clovers, and daisies. And there were wild violets from the woods

and wild geraniums
and wild strawberry blossoms
and yellow star flowers
and blue star flowers
and dogtooth violets
and white violets
and one jack-in-the-pulpit
and another buttercup
and three kinds of clover.

45

How the Animals Took a Bath

ONCE THERE WAS a little boy who didn't know how to take a bath. He had never had a bath because his big fat mother was so busy all day scrubbing white clothes that at night she forgot to scrub her little boy.

One day the little boy came to his big fat mother, and he said:

"Mother, I am one dirty little boy. I have jam on my face and chocolate on my knee. I have mud all over my feet and between my toes from walking down the wet, muddy road. I have dust in my hair from the wind blowing yesterday, and I have dirt all over me from all the time. I think I want to take a bath."

"Well, little boy," said his mother, "run along and take a bath."

"Only I never had a bath," said the little boy. "I don't know how to take one."

But his big fat mother was so busy scrubbing the white clothes that she didn't have time to stop and show her little boy how to take a bath. She just said:

"Run along, little boy, and see how the animals take their bath, because I have to wash all these white clothes before dark."

So the little boy started down the road to see how the animals took a bath. He walked on down the road till he saw a little bird sitting on the branch of a tree.

"Little bird," said the boy, "I am dirty and I want to take a bath, only I don't know how. So I have come to watch you take a bath."

The little bird just sat on the branch of the tree. The little boy sat under the tree and waited to see if the bird would take a bath. The sun was shining warm on the road and on the mud puddles in the road from the last night's rain. The road was warm in the sunshine.

"Just the day for a little bird to take a bath," thought the little boy as he waited and waited.

Pretty soon the little bird began to flutter, and began to ruffle up and flutter its feathers. Then it

46

flew off the tree and dove straight into the mud puddle. It hopped around the edge a little, and then, stomach first, it sank into the shallow part of the puddle and shook itself so that the water splashed all over its back and wings. It made a quick winged fluttering noise. *Flitter, flutter, flitter, flutter.* Then it hopped out on the sand in the road and shook some more. *Whirrrrr.* It flapped its wings.

The little boy watched carefully. But the bird wasn't finished. After shaking and shaking and smoothing its feathers down with its bill, it suddenly began to flutter about in the sand with its wings

stretched out, until it was all sandy. Then it shook and shook itself again and bent its head and smoothed out its feathers and flew away.

"So!" thought the little boy, "this is the way to take a bath." And he ran out in the middle of the road and lay on his stomach in the mud puddle. He wiggled about and he splashed the muddy water all over him. Then he got out and rolled in the sand by the side of the road. But when he got up, he was dirtier than ever.

"Oh, dear," said the little boy, "I'm dirtier than I was before. I guess little boys just don't take baths like birds. I guess I had better go on down the road and find some other animals."

So he walked on down the road until he came to a farm. There by the side of the road was the farmer's pigpen with six dirty little pink pigs in it and a big black pool of water.

"Shoo, little pigs, take a bath," shouted the boy. "Shoo, little pigs, take a bath so that this dirty boy can learn how to get clean."

Just then, two of the little pigs went into the pool and wallowed about in its black edges. The boy didn't even wait for them to come out. He jumped the fence and got right into the black, muddy pool

and rolled around squealing with the little pigs. The water and mud was so cool and soft, the boy was sure that this was the only way to take a bath. But when he got out, he was dirtier than ever. He was all covered and black and sticky with mud.

"Oh, dear," said the little boy, "this must not be the way for a boy to take a bath," and he walked on down the road, dirtier than he had ever been before.

After a while he came to a small white house. There on the front porch sat an old yellow cat, licking her paw and then brushing her wet paw against the side of her face. The boy stood and watched her. Then he licked his hand and rubbed it on his cheek, and he licked his other hand and rubbed it on his ear and he licked his hand and rubbed it on his neck. His hands were getting cleaner.

"Oh, shucks," said the boy, "this sure is the way to take a bath."

Through the doorway of the small white house he saw a mirror hanging in the hall and he ran in to look at his face. But in the mirror his face was dirtier than it had ever been before. He had rubbed all the dirt off his hands on to his face.

"Oh, dear," said the boy as he ran down the road, "I washed like a bird and I washed like a pig, and I washed like a cat, and I'm dirtier than I ever was before. How will I ever learn to take a bath and be a clean little boy?"

Way down the road he came to a green field with brown shining horses galloping and frisking about in the sunshine. He had never seen such smooth shining horses. And beyond the green field with the shining horses was a big white barn.

"Those horses are certainly clean," thought the little boy, "clean and shining." And he wished that he was clean and shining and running about the green fields.

He went up to the big white barn and stood in the doorway. Two men with brushes were cleaning a horse. The brushes made *scrape, shsh, scrape, shsh* noises in the horse's coat. The little boy watched them. He watched them stir the brush around the horse's coat until all the gray dirt and dust came out of the hair. He watched them take a yellow shiny bristle brush and brush away all the dirt that the iron brush had stirred up. There the horse stood, smooth and brown and clean. And he watched them lead the horse out of the stable and into the field. As soon as they were out of sight, he grabbed the sharp iron brush and he rubbed it over one of his muddy legs. Ouch! The sharp ends scratched him and just made white lines in the dirt on his leg.

"Oh, dear, what shall I do?" said the little boy. "I've washed like a bird, and I've washed like a pig, I've washed like a cat, and I've washed like a horse, and still the dirt will not come off."

So the little boy went back to his big fat mother, dirtier than he had ever been before. His mother was just pulling the last piece of white clothes out of the big soapy tub of water when her little boy came home.

"I declare, little boy," she said, "you are dirtier than I have ever seen you before. Didn't you learn from the animals how to get clean?"

"I washed like a bird, and I washed like a pig, I washed like a cat, and I washed like a horse, Mother, and each time I just got a little bit dirtier than I had ever been before."

"You are no bird, little boy, you are no pig, you ain't no cat, and you ain't no horse. How is it that you didn't figure that out? How is it that you didn't find out how little boys take a bath?"

And she turned on the water and grabbed him by the back of his neck and put him right into a big soapy tub.

"I guess it's your mother who will have to show you how to get clean." And so she scrubbed him and scrubbed him all slippery with soap. And when he came out of his mother's tub, he was cleaner than a bird, he was cleaner than a pig, he was cleaner than a cat. And he was cleaner than a horse. He was clean and shining, like a clean little boy.

Said a Fish to a Fish

Said a fish to a fish,
"Look away up high.
What is that shadow
Under the sky?
That great dark shadow sailing by,
Over the ocean,
Under the sky."

Said a fish to a fish,
"That shadow up high
Is a yellow fish
With a yellow eye
That goes swimming along
Under the sky."

"Come, little fish,
Let us fly fly fly
Up where that shadow is
Under the sky."

So up they swam,
Away up high

Where they could see
With their fishes' eye
The great dark shadow sailing by,
The slow dark shadow
Under the sky.

But the slow dark shadow
Under the sky
Was no yellow fish
With a yellow eye.

For they could see
With their fishes' eye
That the slow dark shadow
Under the sky
Was a fishing boat
Sailing,
Sailing by
Over the ocean
Under the sky.

"Come, little fishes,
Fly fly fly,
Fly from that fishing boat
Under the sky,
Come down in the ocean
Away from the sky."

And the fishing boat sailed by.

The Bluefish

A fisherman went fishing,
Went fishing for a fish.
He went fishing for the bluefish
That swims down below.
Jerk Jerk Jerk
Went the fisherman's line,
Pull Pull Pull
His line pulled so.

Ho Ho Ho
Can this be the bluefish
That swims down below?

He pulled in the fish
On the hook on his line
And he looked at the fish
On the hook on his line,
Then the fisherman said,

No
This is just a yellow fish
And I will let him go
So
He let the fish go.

Then the fisherman went fishing
For another fish,
He went fishing for the bluefish
That swims down below.

He caught red fish and green fish
And fast fish and slow,
But he never caught the bluefish
That swims down below.

The Polite Little Polar Bear

ONCE THERE WAS a polite little polar bear who lived in the wide icy regions of the Far North. He lived in a cave of ice in the frozen snow.

This little polar bear had a delightful manner with the fish he ate. "Please, little fish, may I eat you up?" he would say; and the fish were so surprised at such lovely manners in a polar bear that they were frozen with surprise, and the polite little polar bear fished them out from under the ice with one curving swoop of his long fur paw. Then off he loped across the ice on his fur-soled feet, growling happily to himself with his belly full of fish.

One day when the little polar bear was out walking, he met an angry old seal and three rude walruses.

"Bah to you!" said the angry old seal.

"Boo to you!" said the three rude walruses.

But the little polar bear, the polite little polar bear, said, "How very delighted I am to meet three rude walruses and an angry old seal all in one morning!"

"Bah to you, Little Polar Bear," said the angry old seal.

"Boo to you," said the three rude walruses, and shuffled along on their way across the frozen ice to look for fish.

"Unfortunately, Old Seal," growled the polite little polar bear, "I am not very hungry today, so I regret that I will not be able to eat you this minute. But I look forward very much to meeting you again." And the little polar bear went on his way across the frozen ice.

It was such a beautiful icy summer's day, the polite little polar bear felt like a good fifty-mile swim before supper. So when he got to the edge of the great green waters, he slipped from the ice in a walloping dive and swam away off across the icy sea. He rolled through a floating sea meadow of tiny green water plants that grow in the arctic sea, and he batted at some sea butterflies, the kind whales eat. Then he swam on and on through the summer sea, past big ice cakes all white and shining.

He swam and he swam the way polar bears swim miles and miles in the arctic sea for the fun of it; and then suddenly the little polar bear was sleepy, and he wanted to take a nap. But where to

I'm terribly sleepy, and I'm not very old. And as I said before, this water is cold."

But the little baby iceberg just floated right where it was in the arctic sea. Right in the polite little polar bear's way.

"Little Baby Iceberg, if I weren't so polite, I would duck you in the water where you couldn't see the light. Oh, bother!" said the polar bear. "Why am I so polite?"

But the little iceberg stayed right where it was in the arctic sea. All this time the little polar bear was getting sleepier and sleepier, so he just swam right around that silly little iceberg; and there on the other side was the flat ice and a nice fat seal sound asleep for his supper. So he politely ate the seal without even waking it up. He ate sixty pounds of seal before he was full, and then he fell asleep under the midnight sun, looking like a fat little lump of white snow on the rest of the white snow, in the wide icy regions of the Far North.

take it? He was many miles from the flat fields of ice he had come from, and he was in a hurry to get to sleep. So he turned around; and with just his nose out of the water, he swam as fast as he could back towards the ice flats and his own icy cave. He was in an awful hurry to get to sleep.

All of a sudden there was a very small iceberg, just a baby iceberg, in front of him. It was too steep to climb up on; and the little polar bear was in such a hurry, he didn't feel like swimming around it. The little iceberg went too deep down into the water for him to swim under it. So he said:

"Please, Little Iceberg, get out of my way. If you will be so kind, get out of my way."

But the little baby iceberg just floated right where it was in the arctic sea. Right in the polite little polar bear's way.

"Please, Little Iceberg, the water is cold, and

Wind in the Corn

I heard the wind in the corn one day,
I knew that it came from far away,
And it rustled the trembling corn to say
That it was going far away
And could not stay,
Could never stay.

The Green Wind

The green wind blew
And the rains came down
And the animals scurried
Right out of the town.

The green wind blew
And it blew the bees
Right out of their flowers
And up in the trees
And it blew the leaves
Right up in the sky
To turn and whirl
And fall and die.

And the bees in the branches
Began to cry
Oh buzzzz for the flowers
And buzzzz for the earth.
And the wind blew backwards in its mirth
And the wind blew backwards
Through the trees
Till the rain came down
And pushed down the bees,
The swift green wind
With rain.

55

So Many Nights

So many nights.
Blue nights,
Brown nights,
And the sudden lights
In deep black nights
Of stars
And cars
And airplanes
And soft gray nights when it rains
And blue nights with a foggy moon
Smoking in the trees

And pink and red nights
Above great cities
And silver nights all filled with stars
And misty nights when a white mist
Drifts
And lifts over the white-topped fields
And purple nights beyond the lights
Of your own room
And blue snowy nights
And night that is just
Dark bright night.

56

Eyes in the Night

The moon came up on a summer's night
That was soft and dark except for the light
Of fireflies and the gleaming eyes
Of green-eyed cats and the amber eyes of
    wandering dogs
And the red eyes of frogs and the eye of the
    toad
Picked up by lights coming down the road,
Little emerald eyes, the gleaming eyes,
And the eyes of rabbits and foxes
And more and more flickering fireflies.
Then the car went by, and soon
There was only the light
Of a big warm moon
All over the summer night.

The Little Girl's
Medicine

ONCE UPON A TIME there was a little girl who lived way out in the country on a big tobacco farm. She had no brothers and sisters. She had no one to play with, this poor little girl, and she had to play all by herself. She played all by herself year after year and talked to her parents when they ate their meals.

One day, after a while, the little girl became sick. No one knew what was the matter. It was in late August, when they hitched up the two black mules and hauled the tobacco plants away to the big drying barns. But the little girl didn't want to go with them and drive the two big mules. She just sat.

That night there was peach ice cream for dinner, but the little girl didn't want any. She just sat. When it was time to go to bed, she didn't even care.

"Oh dear," said her mother to her father, "our little girl is sick. She loves to drive the two black mules when they haul the tobacco from the fields to the barns, and yet she wouldn't go. She just sat. And she loves peach ice cream, but she wouldn't eat it tonight. She just sat. And she didn't even want to stay up and play when it was time to go to bed. Our little girl must be sick."

So they took the little girl to the doctor in the big city.

The little girl's mother said to the doctor in the big city, "Doctor, my little girl is very sick."

"What is the matter with your little girl?" asked the doctor. "Has she a sore throat?"

And the little girl's mother said, "Doctor, my

little girl doesn't want to drive the mules with the tobacco loads any more, and she doesn't like peach ice cream any more, and she doesn't care whether it is bedtime or whether it isn't bedtime. So I fear that she must be a very sick little girl."

"What!" said the doctor. "Doesn't like peach ice cream! This is serious! Little girl, stick out your tongue."

So the little girl stuck out her tongue, and the doctor looked at it very carefully. "It is a perfectly good tongue that you have in your head, little girl," said the doctor. "Let me see your throat, little girl. Say Ahhhhhhhh."

So the little girl leaned her head way back, way back, and opened her mouth so wide that she looked like a baby robin asking for food. The doctor took a flashlight and peered down into the little girl's throat. "Say Ahhhhhhh," he said.

Then he said, "Little girl, let me feel your pulse," So he held the little girl's wrist in his hand, and with his fingers he listened very carefully, count-ing the beats of the little girl's heart that he could feel in the veins of her wrist. It's a perfectly good heart that you have in you, little girl; but if you don't like to play any more and don't like peach ice cream any more, you are very sick. It would be a pity if your brothers and sisters caught what is wrong with you."

"But I have no brothers and sisters," said the little girl.

"But your cousins and friends might catch it," said the doctor.

"Only I haven't any cousins, and I haven't any friends," said the little girl.

"Then the small animals on the place might catch it," said the doctor.

"There aren't even any small animals," said the little girl, "Not even a little pig. Just two big old black mules that kick every time any one goes near them."

"Well," said the doctor, "this is serious. I will have to prescribe something to make you well."

The doctor sat there for a long time nodding his head, while the little girl and her mother waited. Then he got up and walked around the room three times. Then he opened a book and read three pages of it. Then he coughed three times and he said:

"Little girl, I have just the thing that will make you well." So he picked up a pen and wrote something down on a piece of paper, folded the paper, and handed it to the little girl's mother.

"If you will have this prescription filled," he said to the little girl's mother, "and give it to your little girl right away, I am sure that she will get well."

So the little girl's mother folded up the prescription in her purse without looking at it, thanked the doctor, and went out of his office with the little girl.

"We will go right to the drugstore first thing," said the little girl's mother, "and have this prescription filled before lunch." So they went into the drugstore next door, and the little girl's mother handed the prescription to the druggist, still folded up as the doctor had given it to her.

The druggist was an old man, and he unfolded it slowly.

"Hmmmmp," he said. Then he said it again. "Hmmmmp! Do you expect me to fill this prescription?"

"Why, of course," said the little girl's mother. "Haven't you got that kind of medicine?"

Then the druggist, old as he was, just threw back his head and hollered with laughter. "Do you know what this prescription says?" he asked.

The little girl's mother took the prescription and read it. And this is what the prescription said—

"I have filled prescriptions for thirty years," laughed the druggist, "but never a prescription for a puppy dog. But wait!" he said. "Wait a minute. I think that I can fill this prescription after all. Right across the street. Will you come with me?"

So the little girl and her mother followed the druggist, still chortling and laughing to himself, out the door and across the street to a house that had a back yard.

The little girl and her mother followed him right into the back yard, and there in a box was one furry little puppy dog all by himself.

"This is the last one left," said the druggist. "They belong to my sister, and she is giving them away. So if the doctor says the little girl needs a puppy, this is how we can fill the prescription for her."

"My puppy?" asked the little girl. "All mine?"

"Yes" said the druggist. "That is your puppy if you want him, and you can take him right along home with you this minute."

The little puppy wiggled and jumped around the little girl as if he was just as glad as she was that they would have each other to play with. He had been sitting all by himself in that empty box, just one little puppy all by himself for two long days. He hadn't even eaten the milk that was still in his saucer.

60

So the little girl took her puppy right home with her. They got back just as the big wagon with the two black mules was going out of the gate. The little girl's father was driving.

"Hey, little girl," he called, "do you want to go out after the last load with me?"

"Indeed I do!" said the little girl. "And look what I am going to bring with me!"

She jumped out of the car with the puppy under her arm and climbed up on the wagon beside her father.

"For goodness sakes!" he said. "What in the world have you got there?"

"This," said the little girl, "is my medicine, and I feel much better already."

"Well, come here, Medicine," said the little girl's father. "Are you going to learn to be a good tobacco farmer like me and the little girl?"

Little fat Medicine (for that was the puppy's name from then on) wiggled right up in her father's arms and licked him on the nose, and they all drove along on the wagon together behind the two black mules. They hauled the last load of tobacco on to the wagon and hauled it away to the big tobacco drying barns and hung it up on the racks to dry. It was hard hot work. And then they went home to supper.

And what do you think they had for dessert, and the fat little puppy had a spoonful of it, too? Peach ice cream.

And that night when it was time to go to bed, up the steps scampered the little girl, and up the steps scampered the little puppy. And they both scampered right into the little girl's room. And together that night the little girl and her Medicine went right off to sleep, all curled up in their warm little beds in the same room.